This book is to be returned on or before t[...]

SOMERS PARK PRIMARY SCHOOL

Collins

Look out for more *Jets* from Collins

Jessy Runs Away • *Best Friends* • **Rachel Anderson**
Ivana the Inventor • *Ernest the Heroic Lion Tamer* • **Damon Burnard**
Two Hoots • *Almost Goodbye Guzzler* • **Helen Cresswell**
Shadows on the Barn • **Sarah Garland**
Nora Bone • *Nora Bone and the Tooth Fairy* • *Clever Trevor* • *The Mystery c*
Lydia Dustbin's Diamonds • **Brough Girling**
Thing on Two Legs • *Thing in a Box* • **Diana Hendry**
Desperate for a Dog • *More Dog Trouble* • **Rose Impey**
Georgie and the Dragon • *Georgie and the Planet Raider* • **Julia Jarman**
Cowardy Cowardy Cutlass • *Free With Every Pack* • **Robin Kingsland**
Mossop's Last Chance • *Mum's the Word* • **Michael Morpurgo**
Hiccup Harry • *Harry Moves House* • **Chris Powling**
Rattle and Hum, Robot Detectives • **Frank Rodgers**
Our Toilet's Haunted • **John Talbot**
Rhyming Russell • *Messages* • **Pat Thomson**
Monty the Dog Who Wears Glasses • *Monty's Ups and Downs* • **Colin West**
Ging Gang Goolie, it's an Alien • *Stone the Crows, it's a Vacuum Cleaner* •
Bob Wilson

First published by A & C Black Ltd in 1993
Published by Collins in 1996
10 9 8 7 6
Collins is an imprint of HarperCollins*Publishers*Ltd,
77–85 Fulham Palace Road, Hammersmith, London W6 8JB

ISBN 0 00 674512 1

Text © Brough Girling 1993
Illustrations © Tony Blundell 1993

The author and the illustrator assert the moral right to
be identified as the author and the illustrator of the work.
A CIP record for this title is available from the British Library.
Printed and bound in Great Britain by
Caledonian International Book Manufacturing Ltd, Glasgow

Chapter One

Morning all. Nora Bone, Police Wonder Dog*, at your service.

She doesn't look much like a police dog.

Maybe she's in the Plain Clothes Division!

*Because some people 'wonder' if I'm really a police dog!

As you can see, I'm a rather fine example of a police dog.

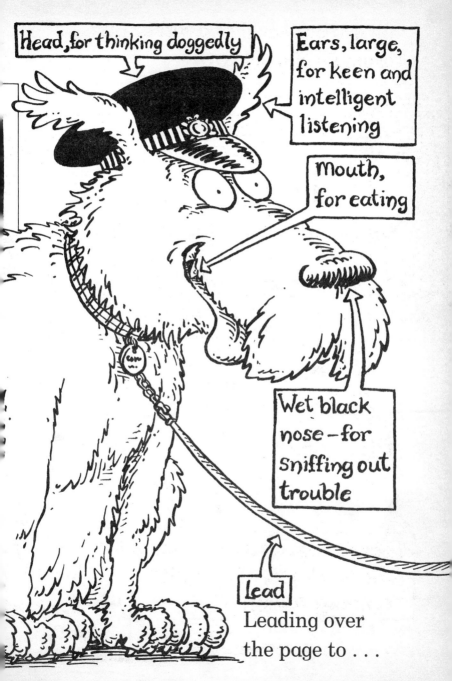

Head, for thinking doggedly

Ears, large, for keen and intelligent listening

mouth, for eating

Wet black nose – for sniffing out trouble

Lead
Leading over the page to . . .

5

. . . my partner,
Police Officer Sally Jenkins.
She's a dog's best friend.
She's kind and loyal,
and she's always
so pleased to
see me.

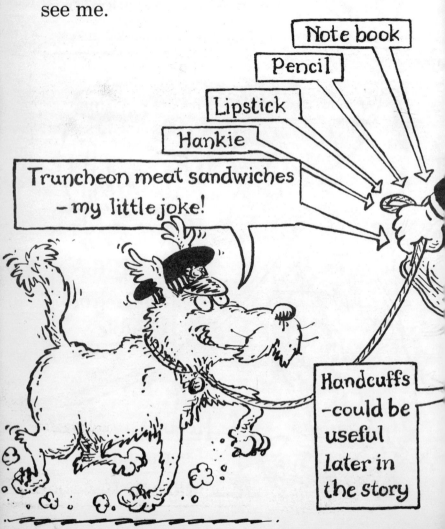

I can tell what she's thinking just by looking at her face.

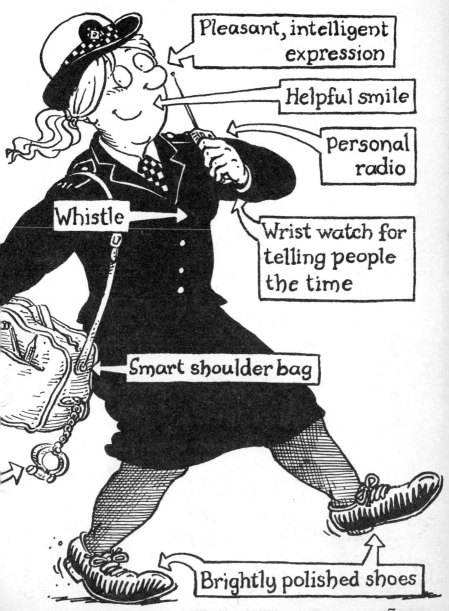

Pleasant, intelligent expression

Helpful smile

personal radio

Whistle

Wrist watch for telling people the time

Smart shoulder bag

Brightly polished shoes

The first thing Sally does when we get to the police station in the morning is to open all my wonderful fan mail:

Dunmarchin
Little Bellering
Wilts.

Dear PC Jenkins,
Please keep your ghastly
dog off my lawn.
Yours sincerely,
Col. Carruthers-Smith.

The Laurels,
Barking Lane,
Wolds.
Dear Madam,
If your dog chases
my cat once more,
I'll call the police, and
that means YOU!!
Fred Jones.

Then we get on with our police work.

We go up to the Chief Inspector's room. He's very important, and I'm sure he's going to thank us for all the good work we've been doing.

They talk about this and that – pretty dull stuff – so as an alert member of the force, I seize the opportunity to do a bit of investigating.

I decide to check through the Chief's wastepaper basket –

you

never

know

what you

might

find.

14

15

However, your dog is another matter. I've got a full-time secretary out there writing creepy, apologetic letters to members of the public who have had their vegetable gardens dug up . . .

I was under the Chief's desk while they were chatting away, and for a moment I thought I'd found something very suspicious in the Chief's briefcase.

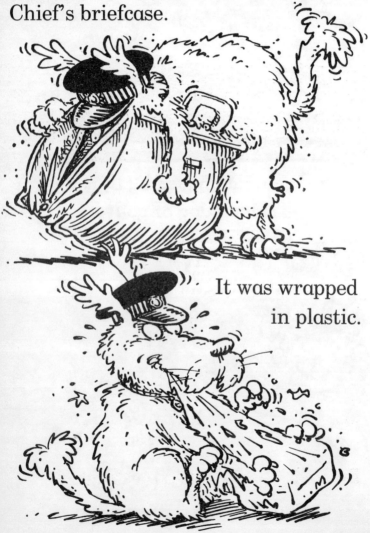

It was wrapped in plastic.

Perhaps it was a bomb!

Bravely I decided to investigate it
by myself.

Luckily it just turned out to be some sandwiches. One was cheese and ham and the other was cold roast beef. Delicious!

Quivering moustache

Cold roast beef

Cheese and ham

I knew Sally would be pleased that I'd checked these things out.

You can never be too careful with suspicious packages.

Today however, I have had a letter which may give you one last chance to show that this dog of yours deserves a place in today's modern and caring police force.
I'll read it to you.
Crossed fingers
Knees knocking

St Hilda's Primary School

Dear Chief Inspector,

Next Saturday we have our annual summer fête and sports' day. It's a very big occasion for the school, with races and games, and lots of fund-raising activities like side stalls, tombola, competitions etc.

We've been having a little trouble at the school lately with certain children, and I'm most concerned that our fête is a success, and nothing goes wrong.

The staff feel that it would be a good idea to have an officer with us during the day, especially since valuable things like the school's silver trophies will be out on display. Maybe if we had an officer who was accompanied by a friendly police dog it would look less official and the children would enjoy meeting them both.

If you are in agreement we would be delighted if the officer could come up to school to meet us on Friday before the fête.

I look forward to hearing from you.

Yours sincerely,

Pat Pugh

Mrs Patricia Pugh
Head Teacher

While Sally was listening to the Chief, I found what I thought was one of his pencils on the floor.

It wasn't very sharp, so I decided to sharpen it for him with my teeth.

But I wasn't very successful.

25

And she yanked me out of the room
– a bit roughly I thought!

Chapter Two

A couple of days later Sally put me
in our police car and we went up to
St Hilda's Primary School.

When Sally had parked the car
she gave me a good talking to!
She's so sweet!

Now look here, Nora, we're here to
meet the staff and children before
tomorrow's sports' day and fête. It's
important that you behave really well.
I don't want you making a fool of
yourself, or messing about, or being
silly. You understand?

I gave my tail
a jolly good wag,
as if to say,

'Don't worry Sal!
You can count
on me!'

She gave me a worried look, and off
we went into the school assembly.

I don't know if you've ever had trouble with a very slippery, well polished, school hall floor.

It's really tricky with four legs

sort of

when three of them

I must say the children seemed
very pleased to see me.

The teacher had rather a lot to say,
and it was ages

blah...blah...
blah...blah...

blah...blah...

before she got

blah...blah...
blah...blah...

round to us.

Now children – this is Police Officer Sally Jenkins and her police dog, Nora Bone. They're going to look after us at the fête tomorrow, and I expect you all to make them feel very welcome.

Now, on to some more important announcements concerning tomorrow . . .

It was at about this time that I noticed that one of the children at the end of the front row had some very interesting looking sweets.

I love sweets, so I wagged my tail in her direction and she soon got the message.

I'd never
actually
bitten
straight
into a

SHERBET FIZZ BOMB before.

aaaaaaaaaAA

PHEWWWW!! I've tried some
pretty weird things in my time, but
this was like eating a firework . . .

. . . I certainly caused quite a stir.

In the end, Sally had to use her whistle to calm the children down, and one of them kindly brought me a bowl of water.

The teacher got on with the rest of her speech.

So don't be late. Remember that people with cakes for the cake stall must report with them to Mr Soper, and Jenny Fielding will have her pony and donkey on the other side of the football posts after three o'clock for rides. Anyone entering a rabbit in the rabbit show must bring it in its hutch, by lunchtime.

I pricked up my ears at the sound of rabbits. I really like rabbits! I *love* the way their little tails bob up and down when they run away.

As we were going out of the school
gates I noticed a suspicious group
of rather evil-looking children
standing on the pavement.

Sally didn't seem to be speaking to
me, so I was able to give the matter
my full attention.

Unfortunately, I couldn't catch what they were saying from the car (though I've got doggishly good hearing).

48

49

Chapter Three

Saturday was a lovely day for a
school fête. There was a bright blue
sky, and no chance of any rain. The
moment Sally and I got there, I knew
we'd have a good time.

BOOKS
From 25p.

The cake stall was absolutely brilliant!

51

While Sally was chatting away to some of the mothers, I inspected the babies in the 'Beautiful Baby' competition.

Why do babies get upset so easily?

And their mothers.
Sally decided it was
time we looked at
the pony riding.

Little did I know what the Nesta Vipers gang were up to.

I've never been very keen on ponies.
They are never very careful where
they PUT THEIR FEET!

One big black and white rabbit was really fast! Everyone seemed to enjoy helping

Wretched dog!

Luckily I just managed to squeeze in after it.

61

Sally soon had handcuffs on the three frightful children. And I must say that everyone was suddenly very nice to me –

- not surprising really, I am a very special dog.

What would we have done without this brilliant police dog?
Cool!!
My hero!
Megatastic Superstardog!
fancy cakes

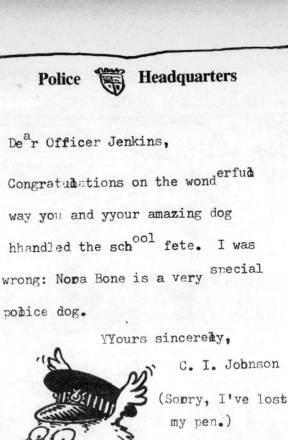

Police 🛡 Headquarters

De^ar Officer Jenkins,

Congratulations on the wond^{erful}
way you and yyour amazing dog
hhandled the sch^{ool} fete. I was
wrong: Nora Bone is a very ^{special}
police dog.

YYours sincerely,

C. I. Johnson

(Sorry, I've lost
my pen.)

CERTIFICATE
OF
MERIT
Nora Bone